Published by Pleasant Company Publications
Copyright © 2004 by American Girl, LLC
All rights reserved. No part of this book may be used or reproduced
in any manner whatsoever without written permission except in the
case of brief quotations embodied in critical articles and reviews.
For information, address: Book Editor, Pleasant Company Publications,
8400 Fairway Place, P.O. Box 620998, Middleton, WI 53562.

Visit our Web site at **americangirl.com**.

Printed in China
04 05 06 07 08 09 10 11 12 LEO 12 11 10 9 8 7 6 5 4 3 2 1

The American Girls Collection®, Nellie™, Nellie O'Malley™, Samantha™,
Samantha Parkington®, and American Girl® are trademarks of American Girl, LLC.

PICTURE CREDITS
The following individuals and organizations have generously given
permission to reprint images contained in "Looking Back":
p. 73—University of Chicago (three orphaned girls); pp. 74–75—Corbis (factory girl);
University of Chicago (three orphaned girls), Kansas State Historical Society, Topeka, KS
(orphan train); pp. 76–77—courtesy of the Orphan Train Heritage Society (newspaper ad
and orphan train children with escorts); Corbis (working-class girls); pp. 78–79—Wisconsin
Historical Society (settlement house cooking class); Jane Addams Memorial Collection,
Special Collections, University Library, University of Illinois at Chicago (children dancing);
© Tom Stewart/Corbis (friends/sisters).

Cataloging-in-Publication Data available from the Library of Congress.

1906
Nellie's
PROMISE

BY VALERIE TRIPP

ILLUSTRATIONS DAN ANDREASEN

VIGNETTES SUSAN McALILEY

American Girl®

THE AMERICAN GIRLS

1764  KAYA, an adventurous Nez Perce girl whose deep love for horses and respect for nature nourish her spirit

1774 FELICITY, a spunky, spritely colonial girl, full of energy and independence

1824 JOSEFINA, an Hispanic girl whose heart and hopes are as big as the New Mexico sky

1854 KIRSTEN, a pioneer girl of strength and spirit who settles on the frontier

1864 ADDY, a courageous girl determined to be free in the midst of the Civil War

1904 SAMANTHA, a bright Victorian beauty, an orphan raised by her wealthy grandmother

1934 KIT, a clever, resourceful girl facing the Great Depression with spirit and determination

1944 MOLLY, who schemes and dreams on the home front during World War Two

FOR TAMARA ENGLAND,
DEAR FRIEND AND TRUSTED EDITOR,
WITH LOVE AND THANKS

TABLE OF CONTENTS

NELLIE'S FAMILY
AND FRIENDS

NELLIE'S FAMILY

UNCLE GARD
*Samantha's generous
uncle, who has taken in
Nellie and her sisters*

AUNT CORNELIA
*Samantha's kind hearted
aunt, who has lots of energy
and newfangled ideas*

NELLIE
*A hardworking girl who
has lost her parents and
is trying to create a
home for her sisters*

SAMANTHA
*Nellie's best friend, who is
also an orphan and who
lives in New York City
with her aunt and uncle*

BRIDGET AND
JENNY
*Nellie's little sisters,
who are seven and eight*

UNCLE MIKE
*Nellie's no-good uncle,
who abandoned Nellie
and her sisters after their
parents' deaths*

MISS BRENNAN
*A teacher at a New York
settlement house and a
good friend to Nellie*

CHAPTER ONE

THE LUCKIEST GIRL

 Nellie O'Malley skipped cheerfully along the city sidewalk. *I am the luckiest girl in New York,* she thought. It was late afternoon, nearly dusk. A strong March wind made Nellie's coat flap and fly out behind her like wings. Nellie tucked the newspaper she was carrying tighter under her arm and snuggled her chin deeper into her collar. She almost enjoyed being cold because she knew that soon she'd be warm and cozy at home.

Home. Nellie smiled. Finally, she and her little sisters, Bridget and Jenny, had a home again. It was a real home, too, where they were safe and loved. For more than a month now, they had been living

1

with Nellie's friend Samantha and Samantha's Uncle Gard and Aunt Cornelia. Nellie thought that Samantha was the best friend anyone could ever have. She was kind and generous. And she was brave, too. Samantha had rescued Nellie and her sisters from Coldrock House for Homeless Girls.

Coldrock House

Nellie shivered as she walked, not from the cold wind, but from the memory of the past sad, scary winter. Back in December, Nellie's mother and father both had died of influenza. Nellie had solemnly promised her dying mother that she would always, *always* keep Bridget and Jenny safe. Nellie had tried hard to keep her promise to Mam. The three girls, still grieving for their parents, had had to go live with their terrible Uncle Mike. He took everything the girls owned, sold it for drink, and then disappeared. The girls were left on their own in the middle of bleak, cold January. Nellie struggled to take care of Bridget and Jenny in Uncle Mike's dirty, dreary apartment, where rats scrabbled in the walls at night and the dark hallways reeked of garbage. But Nellie had no money for food or coal. So, in desperation, the girls ended up at the orphanage. Nellie was just about to be separated from her sisters and sent west on one of the orphan trains when Samantha found the girls and brought them home to Uncle Gard and Aunt Cornelia.

Lamplight spilled out of the windows of the houses Nellie passed. She remembered when she did not even dare to look into those beautiful, warmly lit houses but could only scurry past and imagine what life was like inside. It seemed like a miracle that now she was headed home to a beautiful house herself, bringing Uncle Gard his evening newspaper. Nellie skipped happily. It was a pleasure to be helpful to Uncle Gard and Aunt Cornelia. Nellie loved to go out to do errands for them. Even more, she loved coming home.

Nellie walked past a group of men working on a road crew. Suddenly, one of the men dropped his wheelbarrow full of dirt and paving stones and grabbed Nellie roughly by the arm. "So!" the man growled in a harsh voice. "I found you."

Nellie's heart stopped. It was Uncle Mike! Nellie had never been so unhappy to see anyone in her life. *Oh, why couldn't Uncle Mike have just disappeared forever?* she thought miserably.

Uncle Mike eyed Nellie's fine coat and boots. "Well, well, look at you," he said. "I'm gone two months and I come back to find you dressed like a rich girl. You and Bridget and Jenny must be living with folks who have lots of money. How lucky. Who are these rich swells, Nellie-girl? And where do they live?"

Nellie was shaking with fear, but she was determined not to tell Uncle Mike anything.

Uncle Mike smiled a nasty smile. His mean eyes narrowed. "All right, you stubborn brat," he said. "Don't tell me. I'll find out for myself. When I do, I'll come and get you and your sisters. I'll take you back to live with me. I've every right to do that, you know. I'll put the three of you to work in the factory so that you can bring your wages home to me."

"No!" Nellie exploded. "Don't you come near us!" And with that, Nellie stomped hard on Uncle Mike's foot, wrenched her arm out of his grasp, and took off running.

Uncle Mike started to chase her, but he stumbled over his wheelbarrow and sprawled onto the sidewalk. The road-crew boss hollered, "Get back to work, O'Malley!" So Nellie got away.

She heard Uncle Mike shout after her, "Run, Nellie-girl! But remember, I'm your uncle. You belong to me!"

You belong to me. The words dogged Nellie as she kept on running, as fast as she could, all the way home. Even after Nellie closed the heavy door to Uncle Gard and Aunt Cornelia's house behind her, she seemed to hear the words. *I'm your uncle. You belong to me.* Nellie shuddered. The words were scary and awful and, worst of all, true.

❧

"Please, please, please," chirped Bridget and Jenny in their clear, fluty voices. "Please read us another page. Just one more."

Uncle Gard laughed. "That's what you said three pages ago!" he protested. "But all right."

Nellie looked up from the pinafore she was hemming for Bridget. It was after dinner, and everyone was gathered in the parlor. Uncle Gard was reading aloud to Bridget and Jenny. They perched snugly beside him in his chair like baby birds safe in a nest. Aunt Cornelia was teaching

Samantha how to play chess. The parlor was warm from a fire in the grate. The gentle golden glow of the lamps lit Nellie's face and cast her soft shadow on the wall behind her. Nellie held back a sigh. She wished all the shadowy troubles of her life were behind her, too—over and done with. It was so lovely to have warm clothes and a full stomach, and to see Bridget and Jenny so happy! If they knew that Uncle Mike had come back, their happiness would be ruined. Uncle Gard and Aunt Cornelia would worry, and Samantha would be miserable. Nellie made up her mind. *I'll keep Uncle Mike a secret,* she decided. *I won't tell anyone that I've seen him.*

Nellie put down her sewing. "Bridget and Jenny," she said in a motherly way, "come along now. I'll give you your baths and put you to bed."

"Oh, please, no!" the two little girls said. They hugged Uncle Gard and turned their faces up to him pleadingly. "We don't have to go yet, do we, Uncle Gard?"

Before Uncle Gard could answer, Nellie said, "Now, girls, do as you are told." Nellie apologized to Uncle Gard. "I'm sorry they're pestering you, sir."

"It's quite all right, Nellie," said Uncle Gard.

"I like being pestered by these two cherubs. And please, you don't have to call me 'sir.' You and I are family now."

Aunt Cornelia added gently, "Gertrude can bathe the girls and put them to bed. You don't have to, dear."

Nellie blushed. Bridget and Jenny had slipped easily into their new lives as beloved little girls in a wealthy household. It wasn't as easy for Nellie. She had worked all her life and was used to being useful. Also, in her heart, Nellie had never truly trusted that this new life would last. Now that Uncle Mike was back, she was quite sure that it wouldn't. She believed that Uncle Gard and Aunt Cornelia wanted to adopt her and her sisters. But Mike O'Malley *was* their real uncle. As he had just reminded her, they belonged to him. Nellie didn't see how Uncle Gard and Aunt Cornelia could stop Uncle Mike from taking them back, as he had threatened to.

Aunt Cornelia tugged the bellpull and Gertrude appeared, ready to take Bridget and Jenny upstairs. Gertrude looked cross and put-upon. Nellie could tell that Gertrude resented being a maid for maids, which is what Nellie and her sisters probably would have been if Samantha had not changed everything.

"Come along, you two," Gertrude said tartly to Bridget and Jenny.

The little girls hugged Uncle Gard even more closely and hid their faces against him.

Nellie chided them. "Now, girls—" she began.

But Samantha stood up. "Bridget and Jenny," she said. "Why don't you come upstairs now, and I will tell you a story while Gertrude gives you your baths."

"Oh, good, a story!" said the two little girls. They adored Samantha. They thought that she was the most wonderful storyteller in the world. Bridget and Jenny kissed Uncle Gard, Aunt Cornelia, and Nellie good night. Then they trotted off happily, hand in hand with Samantha. Grumpy Gertrude left, too.

Nellie bent her head over her sewing, thinking how lucky she was to have Samantha for a friend and sweet Bridget and Jenny as sisters. *Don't you worry, Mam,* she promised. *No matter what happens, I will protect Bridget and Jenny. Even if Uncle Mike takes us away from here, I will work and do whatever I have to do to keep Bridget and Jenny safe and happy, just as I told you I would. I don't know how, but I'll do it.*

❧

"*Pssst,*" whispered Samantha. "Nellie!"

"What?" Nellie whispered back.

Nellie and Samantha were at school, in dancing class. Nellie was bending over backward. She looked at Samantha from under her arm, which she was supposed to be fluttering gracefully over her head like a slender branch in a breeze. Unfortunately, Nellie actually looked more like she was using her arm to swat flies.

Samantha nodded toward Nellie's knee. "Your stocking," she hissed.

Nellie looked. "Oh, no, not again!" she groaned.

Nellie was so thin that the athletic uniform the girls wore for dancing class swam on her. The uniform consisted of a blouse, stiff, black, knee-length bloomers, and over-the-knee stockings. The bloomers were supposed to be fastened under the girls' knees tightly enough

to hold up the stockings. But Nellie's legs were so spindly that her bloomers ballooned loosely and her stockings always drooped. Just now, one of her stockings had fallen down completely and was puddled around her ankle. Nellie yanked it up and tucked it back into the baggy bloomers. But she knew it was no use. Sure enough, the stocking was soon droopy again. For the rest of class, Nellie did a dance of *droop and yank, droop and yank* with her stocking.

"It's not your fault," Samantha said as the girls sat down to lunch after dancing class. "Those bloomers are too big for you. Ask Uncle Gard and Aunt Cornelia to buy you a smaller pair."

"Oh, no," said Nellie. Uncle Gard and Aunt Cornelia had given her so many things already! She couldn't ask for more. "Those bloomers are brand-new."

"They may be new," said Samantha, "but they just don't fit you at all."

"I'm afraid that I just don't fit in that dancing class at all," said Nellie, smiling but shaking her head. "That kind of dancing seems so silly to me. I can't see the use of pretending that I'm a tree."

"Oh, well," said Samantha lightly. "Not everything has to have a use, does it? It's all right to learn something just because it's pretty or because it helps you express how you feel. Isn't it?"

"Well, yes, I guess so," Nellie agreed. "It's just that . . ."

Nellie didn't finish her sentence. She didn't know how to tell Samantha that now that Uncle Mike was back, everything had changed for her. Now Nellie felt an urgency about learning real things, practical things, so that she could get a good job someday and earn enough money to take care of her sisters. If Uncle Mike ripped her and her sisters away, Nellie did not want to have to work in a factory for the rest of her life. Only last week, classes in fluttery-arm dancing had made Nellie laugh. Now they made her *impatient.* They seemed like a dangerous waste of time.

But it would be ungrateful to say so, just as it would be unfriendly to tell Samantha that she didn't think she fit in with the other girls at school. Bridget and Jenny studied at home with a tutor, but Uncle Gard and Aunt Cornelia had enrolled Nellie in Samantha's school. Nellie looked fondly at her friend. Samantha was so good-hearted and accepting that she could not see that the other girls at school didn't know what to make of Nellie. They couldn't figure out whether Nellie was Samantha's maid or Samantha's sister. Nellie didn't really blame the girls for their confusion. She was confused about who she was, too! But there was *no* doubt that there was a gap between Nellie and the girls at school. Their lives had been so different.

"My birthday is coming up in two months," Samantha joked to Nellie as they sat at a lunch table with some other girls. "I'll ask for smaller bloomers for you!"

"Thanks!" said Nellie with a grin.

"Those hideous bloomers," groaned a girl named Louisa. "For my birthday, my parents are taking me up in a hot-air balloon. I'd like to toss my bloomers over the side and never see them again!"

"Oh, we went up in a hot-air balloon for my birthday when I turned eight," said a girl named Tissie. "You'll love it."

"When I was eight, my parents gave me a pony," said Louisa. She turned to Nellie and asked politely, "What happened on your eighth birthday?"

"Well," Nellie answered honestly, "that was

when I was working in the thread factory, so I don't think we really celebrated my birthday that year."

"Oh," said Louisa, turning rather pink in the face.

An awkward silence settled over the table. The other girls had never even been inside a factory. Working in one was beyond their imagining.

Samantha piped up, "Let's not talk about when we were eight. It's lots more interesting to talk about what we're going to be when we grow up."

"You're right," said Louisa heartily. "I want to be a dancer, like Isadora Duncan." She fluttered her arm, just as the girls had learned in dancing class. She fluttered her eyelashes, too, which made all the girls laugh.

"I'm going to marry a duke, like Consuelo Vanderbilt did," sighed Tissie. "I'll live in a castle with lots of dogs."

"I either want to be a painter, like *Isadora Duncan* Mary Cassatt," said Samantha, "or the first woman president of the United States." She turned and asked Nellie, "What do you want to do?"

"I'll work as hard as I can at the best job I can get," said Nellie with fierce determination. "All I want is to earn enough money to have a little house where I can keep my sisters safe."

Louisa and Tissie exchanged a glance. Samantha looked bewildered. Nellie realized with a pang that her answer must have sounded odd. It must have sounded as if she and Bridget and Jenny weren't happy at Uncle Gard and Aunt Cornelia's house. Nellie wanted to reassure Samantha that this wasn't what she'd meant, but Nellie could not explain why she had answered as she had. For the rest of their lunchtime, she and Samantha were very quiet.

That evening, Samantha and Nellie were up in their bedroom dressing for dinner. Nellie faced the full-length mirror while Samantha buttoned up the back of Nellie's dress. Around her neck, Nellie wore a silver necklace with a delicate cross, which was the only thing she had left from Mam. *I wish you could see me now, Mam,* thought Nellie. *You'd say I am the luckiest girl in the world.*

Then Samantha said slowly, "Nellie, I know that you and Bridget and Jenny are still very sad about your parents dying."

Nellie nodded. "When Bridget and Jenny wake up at night crying for Mam and Dad, I don't know

I wish you could see me now, Mam, thought Nellie.

how to comfort them. I miss Mam and Dad so much myself," she said.

"Yes," said Samantha gently. "I miss my parents, too." She was thoughtful for a moment. Then she spoke even more gently. "Nellie," she asked, "are you and Bridget and Jenny happy about living here with us?"

Nellie turned quickly to face Samantha. "Oh, yes!" said Nellie with her whole heart. "We love you! You are so kind to us! No one could have been more generous!" Nellie smoothed the front of her dress, the prettiest one she had ever had. "Uncle Gard and Aunt Cornelia have given us more than we ever dreamed of having. And even more important, all of you have made us feel so welcome and at home here." Then Nellie faltered. "I just can't be sure how long . . . That is, I don't know . . ." Nellie could not finish her sentence without spilling the truth about Uncle Mike. Instead she said, "We're so grateful to you. I wish I could *show* you how much in some way. I wish I could *do* something to help Uncle Gard or Aunt Cornelia."

Samantha's face brightened. "I think I understand," she said. "It's what you were saying earlier, about how things should have a use. You want to be *useful*."

"Yes, that's it exactly," said Nellie.

"I have an idea," Samantha said. "Do you know where there's one of those places where they have classes for people who've just come to America, where they teach English and things? I think it's called a settlement house."

"Sure!" said Nellie. "There's a settlement house over by the East River. Bridget and Jenny and I used to go there whenever we could. That's where I learned to sew. And later on, I helped teach people how to use American money. A very nice lady named Miss Brennan was in charge of the settlement house. She used to call me 'Miss Nellie O'Malley-All-Mended' because of the way I could take things apart and put them back together again so that they worked. I liked her very much."

"Well," said Samantha, "I've heard Aunt Cornelia say that she would like to visit a settlement house. Maybe you could take her to the one you know and introduce her to Miss Brennan."

Nellie's face glowed. "Do you really think Aunt Cornelia would like that?" she asked.

"Yes, I do," said Samantha with certainty.

Nellie smiled at Samantha. The idea of going to the settlement house was even more wonderful than Samantha knew. It would make Nellie pleased and proud to be helpful to Aunt Cornelia. And if they went to the settlement house, then Nellie could ask Miss Brennan for advice. Miss Brennan would know what Nellie should learn so that she'd be able to get a job and take care of Bridget and Jenny if Uncle Mike took them away.

"Come on," Nellie said. "Let's go and talk to Aunt Cornelia about the settlement house right now. I'll race you downstairs. Last one down is a pair of baggy bloomers!"

Nellie ran down the stairs with light feet and a lighter heart. Thanks to Samantha's idea, she had true hope for the first time since Uncle Mike's reappearance that she'd be able to keep her promise to Mam.

CHAPTER TWO

THE SETTLEMENT HOUSE

 Nellie and Samantha went straight to the parlor to speak to Aunt Cornelia before dinner. In a rush of words, Samantha presented the idea of going to the settlement house. Aunt Cornelia listened carefully.

Finally, Samantha said, "Nellie says that she will introduce you to Miss Brennan, the lady in charge. Do you want to go?"

"I have wanted to visit a settlement house very much," said Aunt Cornelia. "I think the work that is done there to educate women is so important, and I'd like to help, if I can." Aunt Cornelia turned to Nellie. "Would you like to go back to visit the settlement house, dear?" she asked.

"Oh, yes!" Nellie answered earnestly.

Aunt Cornelia smiled. "Then we'll go tomorrow afternoon after school," she said. "And Nellie, you will lead the way."

Nellie beamed. She loved to be useful!

The next afternoon was cold and sleety, but that did not stop Nellie, Samantha, and Aunt Cornelia from setting forth. The streets in Uncle Gard and Aunt Cornelia's quiet neighborhood were lined with trees, which looked shiny and pretty with sleet coating their branches. But the sleet soon changed to slush, and there were no more pretty trees as Nellie led Samantha and Aunt Cornelia along the much bigger, broader, busier streets on the way to the settlement house.

At the corner of 17th Street—one of the biggest, broadest, busiest streets of all—Nellie paused. She felt as if she were standing at the edge of a raging, rushing river of people. Black umbrellas bobbed above the crowd here and there as hundreds of people jostled one another, pushing their way along, shouting, laughing, and calling out in a singsong symphony of different languages. The sidewalks were clogged with pushcarts piled high with pots and pans, turkeys and hams, or potatoes and fish to sell, so the river of people churned its way down the middle of the street.

"Stay close to me," Nellie told Aunt Cornelia and Samantha as they stepped off the curb and plunged into the crowd. Nellie pushed a path through the people. Whenever she could, she glanced back at Aunt Cornelia and Samantha. She knew that they were not used to such rough and rude commotion. She was afraid they might be overwhelmed. But Aunt Cornelia's eyes were alight with interest, and Samantha grinned gamely. So Nellie forged steadily ahead. She knew she was going in the right direction because the dank, fishy smell of the river was growing stronger and stronger.

Then suddenly Nellie gasped. She stopped so short that Samantha bumped into her. Was that Uncle Mike Nellie saw ahead of them, weaving through the crowd? *Quick,* Nellie thought frantically, *we've got to get out of here before he turns and sees us!*

"What is it, Nellie?" asked Aunt Cornelia.

Nellie was so shaken that she stammered. "I . . .
I think I made a wrong turn," she said. "Please,
come this way. Follow me."

Samantha and Aunt Cornelia followed
trustingly as Nellie ducked down a narrow side
street no wider than an alley. Nellie was relieved to
get away from the man she thought might have been
Uncle Mike. But she had a sinking feeling that grew
worse with every step. This street was not cheerfully
bustling with people, as 17th Street had been. At
first, it seemed to be ominously empty. Then Nellie
saw groups of men slouched in some of the dark
doorways. The men stared at Nellie, Aunt Cornelia,
and Samantha and muttered as they passed. Nellie
ignored them until one man stepped right in front
of her, blocking her way.

Nellie was not about to let the man frighten
Samantha or Aunt Cornelia. She knew how to deal
with bullies after living with Uncle Mike. Nellie
squared her shoulders and scowled defiantly at the
man. "Get out of my way, you alley rat!" she
ordered in the meanest voice she could muster.

She heard Aunt Cornelia and Samantha gasp.
They had never heard Nellie speak in such a way.

The man smirked, but he stepped back.

Nellie motioned to Aunt Cornelia and Samantha. "Please walk on ahead," she said.

Aunt Cornelia hesitated, but Samantha pulled her by the arm.

Nellie stood with her hands on her hips and glared at the man until he shrugged and went back to his doorway. Only then did she scurry to catch up to Samantha and Aunt Cornelia. She hoped they were not upset. She worried that bringing them to this part of the city was not such a good idea after all.

Luckily, the settlement house loomed ahead at the next corner. The big gray building looked sturdy and solid and as welcome as a safe harbor.

"Here we are," said Nellie as they walked up the steps. She did not say, "At last." But she thought it, and she could tell Samantha and Aunt Cornelia were thinking it, too.

Aunt Cornelia took a deep breath once they were inside. "Something smells delicious!" she said.

Nellie grinned. "Cooking classes," she explained. "Come with me, please. First, we'll find Miss Brennan. Then I'll show you around."

As they walked down the clean-swept hallways,

every room they passed buzzed with activity. Miss Brennan had an office, but she was hardly ever in it. Nellie knew it was far more likely that they'd find Miss Brennan stirring something up with a cooking class, hammering with a carpentry class, painting with an art class, tossing a ball in the gymnasium, or playing tag with the kindergartners. Sure enough, they found Miss Brennan singing in one of the language classes.

Miss Brennan smiled with delighted surprise and waved to Nellie when she saw her in the doorway. She hurried over to say hello as soon as the song ended.

"Well, if it isn't Miss Nellie O'Malley-All-Mended!" Miss Brennan said, her dark eyes snappy and cheerful. "I'm glad to see you. We've missed you and your hands that are so clever at fixing things. You look well and happy. And how are Bridget and Jenny?"

"Oh, we're all very well and happy, Miss Brennan, thank you," said Nellie, smiling up at the tall young woman. "We live with wonderful friends now. May I introduce them? This is Mrs. Edwards, and this is Miss Samantha Parkington."

"How do you do?" asked Miss Brennan as she shook hands with Aunt Cornelia and Samantha. "I am delighted to meet friends of my friend Nellie."

"Mrs. Edwards would like to help here at the settlement house," said Nellie.

Miss Brennan smiled a wide smile at Aunt Cornelia. "Would you now? That's lovely!" she said. "We're glad to have you. Is there anything in particular you'd like to do, Mrs. Edwards?"

Aunt Cornelia looked uncertain. "I don't really know," she said. "I'm very interested in women's education, but I'm curious about all your classes. It's all so new to me here."

"No worry," said Miss Brennan. "Nellie can show you around and then you can decide where you'd like to help out. You'll find the settlement house is like a very lively school. Our students are all ages. They speak lots of different languages. They're new to this country, and they're eager to learn English, and American customs, and new skills that will help them better themselves. Most of them, grown-ups and children alike, come to their classes here after they've already worked hard for long hours at their jobs." Miss Brennan shook her head.

"There, now. I'm sorry!" she apologized. "I've talked a streak, haven't I? It's a fault of mine."

"Oh, not at all," said Aunt Cornelia.

"It's just that I admire our students so much," said Miss Brennan. "I am so proud of the work they do here. You will admire them, too, once you get to know them, I'm sure."

"I'm sure I will," said Aunt Cornelia.

"I'll leave you in Nellie's hands now," said Miss Brennan. "She can be your guide." Miss Brennan smiled at Nellie and gave her a hug. "You're a good girl to come back to see me, after your life's so changed for the better," she said. "Someday you and I will have a nice long sit-down over a cup of good Irish tea, so you can tell me everything that has happened since I saw you last."

"Oh, yes, I'd love that!" said Nellie fervently. She was eager to ask Miss Brennan for advice.

"Off with you, then," said Miss Brennan. She nodded to Aunt Cornelia and Samantha. "It was nice to meet you both. Enjoy your visit," she said. And with that, Miss Brennan walked briskly away down the hallway.

Nellie grinned at Samantha and Aunt Cornelia.

"Miss Brennan is probably in a hurry to get to the gymnasium," she said. "She hates to miss dancing class. It's wonderful."

"Wonderful?" asked Samantha. "But I thought you didn't like dancing."

Earnestly, Nellie tried to explain. "The dancing they do here is different from the dancing we do at school," she said. "They don't pretend to be trees here. They dance *real* dances, like waltzes, that people actually do at parties and celebrations and all. Sometimes the students teach dances from the countries they came from. Those are the most fun."

"I don't—" Samantha began to say.

But just then they were passing the kindergarten room. "Oh," Nellie interrupted. "I used to bring Bridget and Jenny here to play. Let's go in. You'll like this, Samantha."

Nellie led Samantha and Aunt Cornelia into the kindergarten room. It was warm and well-lit, with tall windows. The room smelled of paint and clay and was filled with children. They were playing, reading, or talking. The children's clothes were ragged, and some children had dirty bare feet. Many of the children looked tired. It was only when they

smiled that their thin faces looked
bright and childlike. Nellie saw
one little girl who had fallen fast
asleep in a quiet corner, and
another girl who was eating a
piece of bread with more haste

than manners. Nellie's heart went out to the little girls.
It had not been so very long ago, when they had lived
with terrible Uncle Mike, that Bridget's and Jenny's
faces had looked exhausted and pinched, just like the
faces of these children. Nellie was grateful to Uncle
Gard and Aunt Cornelia—and determined that her
sisters would never look like that again.

The stout and kindly teacher, Mrs. VanVorst,
came over to say hello. Nellie introduced her to
Aunt Cornelia and Samantha.

"I miss Bridget and Jenny," said Mrs. VanVorst.
"I remember how much they used to love stories."

"They still do!" said Nellie. "They especially
love the stories Samantha tells them. She is a
wonderful storyteller."

Mrs. VanVorst looked expectantly at Samantha.
"Would you like to tell these children a story, miss?"
she asked.

"Oh, I don't know," said Samantha. She sounded rather shy and unsure.

Nellie knew how it was to feel shy and awkward and out of place. She felt that way at school all the time! To help Samantha feel at ease, Nellie nudged her and grinned. "Go on," she said. "You can tell them one of the stories you tell Bridget and Jenny."

"Well, all right," said Samantha.

Samantha sat down in a rocking chair and the children gathered around her feet. As Nellie and Aunt Cornelia turned to leave the room, they heard Samantha saying, "I'm going to tell you a story about a sailing ship."

"Ahhh!" said all the children eagerly. They scooted up to be nearer to Samantha.

With Samantha settled in the kindergarten, Nellie tried to think of a class that would interest Aunt Cornelia. "Would you like to see one of the cooking classes?" she asked.

"Yes!" said Aunt Cornelia. "I would indeed."

So Nellie led the way to the kitchens. In no time at all, Aunt Cornelia was happily wrapped in a big white apron, her elegant hat still on her head, her

sleeves rolled up, and her arms deep in soapsuds at
the sink. She was helping wash the pots and pans
the cooking students had used. From time to time,
Aunt Cornelia had to wipe her hands dry on her
apron so she could take hold of something one of the
students brought her to taste. Most of the students
were grown-ups, Italian and German ladies. They
were very generous with samples.

"*Mmm*," said Aunt Cornelia after a taste of
fresh-baked bread. "Oh, Nellie, I wish I could say in
Italian and German that the bread is delicious."

Nellie had learned some Italian and German
words when she helped at the settlement house
before. "In Italian you say, '*Il pane é molto buono,*'
and in German you say, '*Das Brot schmeckt gut,*'"
Nellie told Aunt Cornelia. Then she laughed and
said, "But I think '*mmm*' is the same in every
language!"

Nellie loved translating for Aunt Cornelia and
working beside her in the cooking class. The hours
flew by. All too soon it was time to gather Samantha
from the kindergarten classroom and go home. It
was dark and cold and had begun to sleet again
when they came out of the settlement house, and

Aunt Cornelia had to wipe her hands dry on her apron so she could take hold of something one of the students brought her to taste.

Samantha and Aunt Cornelia were tired. Luckily, a horse-drawn cab was passing by. Aunt Cornelia waved to the driver to stop, and they all climbed  inside. Nellie sat in the middle, between Aunt Cornelia and Samantha, as they rode home.

Aunt Cornelia sighed a happy, tired sigh. "Nellie, dear child," she said, "thank you. I've wanted to visit a settlement house for a long time to find out about their classes for women. I'm very grateful to you for helping me do so." Then Aunt Cornelia leaned back against the cushions and closed her eyes.

Clip-clop, clip-clop. Nellie found the sound of the horse's hooves on the pavement very comforting. She was comforted, too, by knowing that they'd be returning to the settlement house. Nellie was sorry that she had not been able to speak to Miss Brennan alone this time, but she was sure she'd have a chance sometime soon, because Aunt Cornelia had decided to help out there once a week. Nellie felt a warm glow of satisfaction knowing that Aunt Cornelia had really liked their visit to the settlement house. Nellie hoped that Samantha had liked it, too.

Nellie looked at Samantha in the faint light of the cab. She was perplexed and alarmed to see that Samantha's eyes were full of tears.

Nellie pulled her lacy handkerchief from her purse and held it out to Samantha. "Samantha," Nellie whispered, "what's wrong?"

Samantha did not take the handkerchief. She turned her face away and looked out the sleet-covered window of the cab. "Nothing," she said shortly. "I'm fine."

But Nellie knew that her friend wasn't fine at all.

* * *

When Samantha came to dinner, Nellie saw that she had washed her face clean of all the traces of her tears. Samantha was subdued, but she smiled as sweetly as usual, especially at Bridget and Jenny. She listened even more attentively than usual to the little girls' merry chatter, and she seemed to study them as if she were meeting them for the very first time. Nellie watched Samantha gently put Jenny's napkin back in her lap and lovingly tuck a wisp of Bridget's hair back behind her ear. Jenny and Bridget and Samantha looked at one another with such affection that Nellie almost felt excluded by the three of them.

Samantha was so distracted by Bridget and Jenny that Aunt Cornelia had to say her name twice to get her attention. "Samantha," said Aunt Cornelia. "Samantha?"

"Oh! Yes?" said Samantha. "I beg your pardon."

Aunt Cornelia smiled. "I was just telling Gard what a wonderful guide Nellie was for us today when we went to the settlement house," she said.

"Oh," said Samantha. Her voice sounded strained. "Yes."

"I am very proud of you, Nellie," said Aunt Cornelia. "Samantha and I never would have found our way to the settlement house through those busy, confusing streets. And you were so brave when you defended us from that rude ruffian!"

"What's this?" asked Uncle Gard. He looked alarmed.

"Nellie defended Samantha and me from a very unsavory character," said Aunt Cornelia. "She faced him down like a brave soldier."

"Well, well," said Uncle Gard. "Thank you, Nellie. But, Cornelia my love, you must promise me that if you go to the settlement house again, you will be sure to take a cab."

"Very well, dear," said Aunt Cornelia. "I intend to go back to the settlement house at least once a week. It's a wonderful place. Nellie introduced us to Miss Brennan, who is in charge there. Then Nellie translated for me with the Italian and German ladies in the cooking class."

Uncle Gard looked astounded. "You can speak Italian and German, Nellie?" he asked.

"Only a little," said Nellie.

"Isn't she a marvel?" asked Aunt Cornelia.

"Absolutely!" said Uncle Gard. He tugged on Nellie's hairbow gently and smiled at her fondly.

Nellie blushed. She felt funny. It was nice to be praised, of course. And she was terribly glad to have pleased Aunt Cornelia. But something was wrong. Nellie was watching Samantha's face, and she saw that Samantha did not look happy. The more Aunt Cornelia talked about their visit to the settlement house, the unhappier Samantha's expression was.

"And Nellie found the perfect place for Samantha," Aunt Cornelia was saying. "She brought Samantha to the kindergarten class and had her tell the children a story." Aunt Cornelia turned to

Samantha. She asked, "Didn't you love being with the children in the kindergarten, Samantha?"

"Yes," said Samantha.

Aunt Cornelia, her eyes bright with enthusiasm, waited for Samantha to say more. But Samantha said nothing.

Instead, Samantha turned away, back to Bridget and Jenny. Nellie caught just a glimpse of Samantha's face. Samantha's eyes were bright, too, but not with enthusiasm. Nellie's heart sank. Samantha was not only unhappy. She was angry, too.

Suddenly, Nellie understood. It was clear that Samantha had *not* liked going to the settlement house. She had disliked it so much that she could hardly bear to speak about it. The more Aunt Cornelia talked about the settlement house and the more Aunt Cornelia praised Nellie, the more Samantha was displeased. It almost seemed as if . . . Nellie swallowed hard. Could it possibly be that Samantha was jealous? Was Samantha angry at *her*?

THE LETTER

 Usually, Nellie loved bedtime at
Uncle Gard and Aunt Cornelia's house.
Every night, after Uncle Gard and Aunt
Cornelia had come in to wish them sweet dreams,
Nellie and Samantha would whisper and giggle and
talk about the day. Sometimes Nellie did the
fluttery-arm dance on their bed and Samantha
laughed so hard that she had to bury her face in
her pillow. Other times Samantha and Nellie had
so much on their minds and talked so long that
Uncle Gard had to come remind them that it was
time to go to sleep. More than once when this had
happened, Uncle Gard had become caught up in
their conversation. Then Aunt Cornelia had to come

find him and remind *him* that it was time for bed!

But the night of their visit to the settlement house, Samantha curled up with her back to Nellie as soon as Uncle Gard and Aunt Cornelia turned off the light and left. Outside, a mournful wind blew. It rattled the windows as if it were trying to get in. Nellie almost wished the wind *would* whoosh through their room. Maybe it could blow away the heavy silence between Samantha and her.

Finally, Nellie sat up in bed and whispered, "Samantha?"

"Yes?" Samantha answered, so softly that Nellie could hardly hear her over the wind.

Nellie asked, "Our trip to the settlement house upset you, didn't it?"

"Yes," said Samantha. "I don't want to talk about it." Her voice sounded as if she was struggling not to cry.

"Oh, Samantha!" Nellie pleaded. "We've always been able to talk about everything before. Please, you've got to tell me what's made you so upset."

Samantha sat up in bed and hugged her knees to her chest. Nellie waited for her to speak. When she did, Nellie was shocked. She had never heard

Samantha's voice sound so angry. "The truth is," Samantha said, "that I *hated*—"

But Samantha didn't finish her sentence, because just then, the door burst open and two small white figures flew through the air, bounced onto the bed, and hid under the covers.

"The wind is scaring us," Bridget's muffled voice wailed. "It's moaning."

"We don't like it," said Jenny. "Can we stay here with you, Samantha?"

"Of course!" said Samantha. All the anger in her voice was replaced by gentleness, indulgence, and love.

After a tremendous amount of wiggling and giggling and many complaints about who had cold feet and who was hogging the pillows, Jenny and Bridget settled down to sleep. Nellie and Samantha could not continue their conversation about the settlement house and risk awakening the little girls. Anyway, it was clear to Nellie that Samantha truly did not want to talk about what was troubling her.

Nellie was awake for a long time that night, worrying and listening to the wind howl. Always before, through good times and terrible times, the one thing that Nellie had been sure of was Samantha's friendship. Now it seemed as if that friendship was in danger.

Partly, it was Uncle Mike's fault. Nellie had always told Samantha everything before. The scary secret about Uncle Mike's reappearance was a wedge that separated her from Samantha. And now today, the separation had grown wider because of their visit to the settlement house. Of course Uncle Gard and Aunt Cornelia meant well, but Nellie wished that they had not praised her so much. Samantha must have thought that Nellie was showing off, trying to push herself between Samantha and Uncle Gard and Aunt Cornelia. Nellie completely understood how even the very best and kindest of friends, which Samantha was, would resent that! Nellie tossed and turned, sleepless and miserable. With all her heart, Nellie wanted to make things right again between herself and Samantha. She just did not know *how*.

The next day, the sky was high and blue and fresh and clear. All traces of the sleet had disappeared. It was Saturday, so Uncle Gard did not have to go to his law office. At breakfast he

announced, "It's a perfect day
for a ride in my new motorcar.
Who'd like to come?"

Bridget and Jenny burst with enthusiasm.

"Oh, please, I would!" said Jenny.

"Me, too! Me, too!" said Bridget.

"I think I'll say no thank you, dear," Aunt
Cornelia said to Uncle Gard. "But Samantha and
Nellie, you two should go. The fresh air will do you
good. You look peaked, both of you. You were
probably up too late talking again, as usual."

Nellie did not meet Samantha's eyes.
Fortunately, Bridget and Jenny demanded
everyone's full attention. They bounced out of their
seats, darted off, and returned with their coats and
Nellie's and Samantha's, too. The big girls had to
help the little girls put on their coats and button
them up before they put on their own. All the while,
Bridget and Jenny were so giddy and gleeful that
their chatter covered up the silence between Nellie
and Samantha. When all four were ready to go, they
skittered out the front door and climbed into Uncle
Gard's motorcar.

Uncle Gard cranked the engine. "Here we go!"

he shouted as he got in and sat behind the wheel.

"Hurray!" shouted the little girls.

The engine sputtered, spewed smoke, and stopped.

Uncle Gard climbed out, cranked the engine again, and climbed back into his seat. "Here we go!" he shouted.

"Hurray!" cheered the little girls.

The engine sputtered, spewed, and stopped again.

Uncle Gard sighed. He climbed out of the motorcar, lifted the hood over the engine, and stared at it with his hands on his hips.

Bridget and Jenny sat still for a while, but soon grew restless. They climbed over into the front seat and both held on to the steering wheel, pretending to drive.

Nellie and Samantha got out of the car and went to stand next to Uncle Gard. Nellie's father had been a driver, and Nellie had spent many happy hours with him, watching him tinker with motorcars. Her father had enjoyed showing her how motorcar engines worked.

"What's the trouble *this* time?" Uncle Gard muttered, mostly to himself.

Nellie spoke up timidly. "It sounded like the carburetor to me," she said. "Do you mind if I take a look?"

Uncle Gard threw back his head and laughed with delight. "By all means," he said. "You're quite a girl, Nellie. What would I do without you?"

Nellie smiled rather weakly at Uncle Gard. She glanced at Samantha to see if, once again, Uncle Gard's praise had upset her. But Samantha had already turned away, so Nellie could not see her face.

"Samantha!" called Bridget. "Get back in! We'll be your drivers. Where do you want to go?"

"Drive me to Mount Bedford, please," said Samantha, playing along with Bridget and Jenny.

"Yes, ma'am!" the two little girls replied, delighted. Bridget and Jenny made engine noises and honking noises as they pretended to drive. They bounced on the seats so wildly that the whole motorcar shook and the hood wobbled over Uncle Gard's and Nellie's heads.

"Bridget and Jenny," said Nellie, "please stop bouncing."

Bridget and Jenny stopped for a moment. But only a moment. In no time, they were bouncing more than ever. Then Bridget honked the horn by mistake, which threw both little girls into gales of laughter.

"Girls!" scolded Nellie, annoyed. "Will you stop your nonsense, please?"

"Nellie, you're such a spoilsport!" grumbled Bridget.

"You are no fun," added Jenny.

"Come on, Bridget and Jenny," said Samantha. "Let's go inside. The three of us can have more fun there. Uncle Gard and Nellie don't want us around here."

"All right!" said Bridget and Jenny agreeably. Immediately, they clambered out of the motorcar.

Nellie poked her head out from under the hood. She watched Bridget, Jenny, and Samantha go inside, laughing and chatting. Nellie had the same funny, left-out feeling she'd had at dinner the night before.

"Bridget, Jenny, and Samantha," Uncle Gard said with a smile. "The gleesome threesome!"

All of a sudden, Nellie felt hurt. Bridget and Jenny liked being with Samantha more than they liked being with her. Now it was Nellie's turn to feel jealous.

20

A few weeks later, on a balmy spring afternoon, Nellie heard Aunt Cornelia calling to her. "Nellie, dear girl! The cab is here," said Aunt Cornelia. "It's time to go."

"Coming!" Nellie answered. She clattered down the stairs, grabbed her coat and hat, and followed Aunt Cornelia to the horse-drawn cab that was waiting outside.

Aunt Cornelia smiled at Nellie when they were settled inside the cab. "Thank you for coming with me to the settlement house, dear," she said. "I do appreciate it."

Nellie smiled. "Oh, I love going with you," she said truthfully.

The settlement house was the one place Nellie felt truly comfortable and useful. She went with Aunt Cornelia twice a week to the settlement house now, usually after school. Samantha always chose to stay at home with the two little girls. That meant that Bridget, Jenny, and Samantha spent more and more time together without Nellie, and Nellie and Aunt Cornelia spent more and more time together without Samantha.

It seemed that as the weather grew warmer, Nellie and Samantha's friendship grew cooler. It hurt Nellie's heart, but she did not know what to do. Though she did not mean to, she seemed to damage her friendship with Samantha more with each passing day. Nellie knew Samantha could see how impatient she was at school with the classes that weren't preparing her to support Bridget and Jenny if they had to live with Uncle Mike. At home, Samantha was always leaving Nellie alone with Uncle Gard and Aunt Cornelia, as if it was too hurtful to Samantha to be with the three of them. And whenever Nellie tried to help Samantha care for Bridget or Jenny, Samantha shooed her away. Just the other morning, Jenny was crying because she missed Mam. Samantha immediately gathered Jenny into her arms and murmured comforting words to her. Nellie felt neither needed nor wanted.

Oh, it was all such a sorry tangle. *Maybe we never*

should have come to live with Uncle Gard and Aunt Cornelia, thought Nellie. *If I had known how it would damage my friendship with Samantha, I wouldn't have. Maybe it would be better if I left.*

Miss Brennan met Nellie and Aunt Cornelia at the door of the settlement house. Miss Brennan threw her arms open wide. "My two favorite helpers!" she said.

"Good afternoon," said Nellie and Aunt Cornelia. They spoke at the same time, then laughed at themselves.

"You had better hurry along, Mrs. Edwards," said Miss Brennan in her brisk, bossy, cheerful way. "They're waiting for you in the cooking class." Miss Brennan put her hand on Nellie's shoulder. "I'm going to borrow Nellie for a while, if you don't mind. I promised her a chat and a cup of tea, and it's high time I kept that promise." Miss Brennan smiled sheepishly. "Also, the clock in my office has stopped. I need the help of 'Miss Nellie O'Malley-All-Mended to fix it," she said.

"Very well," said Aunt Cornelia with great good humor. "I'll do the best I can without Nellie to translate for me."

Miss Brennan led Nellie to her office. Nellie fixed the clock, which really just needed to be wound and oiled. Then Miss Brennan poured them each a cup of tea. "So, then," she said, "I know that a great many things have changed in your life. But I hope you still like shortbread cookies."

Nellie laughed. "Yes, I still do!" she said.

Miss Brennan sat down and sighed. "Oh, it feels good to sit down," she said. "I'm that busy. But as my grandmother used to say, 'We're blessed with work.' And I do feel blessed to have this job."

Nellie sat forward. "I've been wanting to ask you . . . how did you get this job?" she asked earnestly. "Did you have to go to a special school to be trained for it?"

"Well, I was trained to be a teacher," said Miss Brennan. "My parents died when I was young, like you. When I was about your age, I went to a boarding school in Boston, on Beacon Street. It is called the Clark School. There were lots of Irish girls there, just like me. We were eager to be teachers instead of maids or factory workers, as our parents had been.

I studied very hard, and I was very happy at Clark School." She looked at Nellie with an interested expression. "And are you happy at the fine school you're going to now, Nellie?" she asked.

Nellie took a deep breath. "No," she said. "I am not."

Miss Brennan sat back. "I think you had better tell me all about it," she said.

"I feel very ungrateful," said Nellie. "But I don't think the school Samantha and I go to is right for me. It's not preparing me to get a real job, one where I'd earn enough money to take care of Bridget and Jenny the way I promised my mother I would. And I'm going to need a real job because . . ." Nellie hesitated, and then she told Miss Brennan the truth. "You see, I haven't told anyone, but . . . but I ran into my Uncle Mike on the street a while ago. He threatened to come and take my sisters and me away from Uncle Gard and Aunt Cornelia and make us work in the factory again. He'll do it, too. We're just lucky that so far, he doesn't seem to know where to find us."

Miss Brennan sighed a sad sigh that came straight from her heart. "Ah, Nellie," she said. "I'm sorry to have to tell you this. Your uncle was here the other day. Full of bluster and swagger, he was, and ranting and raving and asking questions about you and your sisters."

Nellie shivered. She looked at Miss Brennan wide-eyed.

"You can be sure that I gave him a piece of my mind and sent him on his way," said Miss Brennan stoutly. "I didn't tell him anything about you and your sisters, of course. I wouldn't give a hooligan like that the time of day!"

Nellie tried to keep her hand steady, but her teacup rattled as she set it on the saucer. "Thank you for trying to protect us, Miss Brennan," she said. "But I'm pretty sure Uncle Mike will find us any day now." Nellie shook her head. "I don't see how I can keep my promise to Mam to care for Bridget and Jenny if I'm working in the factory and Uncle Mike is drinking up all the money I earn," she said. "That's what he did when we lived with him before. Then he abandoned us."

After Nellie stopped talking, Miss Brennan was quiet and thoughtful. Then she said, "Well, Nellie, you are a smart, brave girl. You've had to carry more than your share of burdens all by yourself. But now you live with good, kind people who love you. I think you should tell *them* what you have told me. Mrs. Edwards mentioned that Mr. Edwards is a lawyer. He will know about laws that are intended to protect children like you and your sisters, laws that send bad people like your Uncle Mike to jail for abandoning children or mistreating them. I am sure Mr. and Mrs. Edwards will try to help you."

Nellie sighed. "They'll try," she agreed. "But if Uncle Mike comes—"

Miss Brennan leaned forward and took both of Nellie's hands in hers. "Nellie, no matter what happens, you'll have to make a decision," she said. "If your uncle comes and takes you away *or* if you stay with Samantha and her aunt and uncle, it will still be up to you to decide what you want your life to be like and who you want to be. You have to choose the future *you* want, and you have to find a path that'll get you there."

Nellie spoke solemnly. "I think I have decided," she said, nodding. "I decided right now. I want to be a teacher like you when I grow up."

Miss Brennan gently squeezed Nellie's hands. "That's the finest compliment I've ever had," she said. She stood up, saying, "But get away with you now, before you turn my head with your compliments! Mrs. Edwards will be needing you to translate for her."

Nellie handed Miss Brennan her teacup and saucer. "Thank you for the tea," she said. "And thank you even more for your help."

"Thank you for mending my clock," said Miss Brennan. "Here's payment for you." Miss Brennan handed Nellie a coin. "It's an old Irish coin," she explained, "too old to use to buy anything. But maybe it'll remind you of your family's past while you're on your way to your future."

"Oh, Miss Brennan," said Nellie. "I'll keep it with me always."

"Good," said Miss Brennan. She smiled. "I'm proud of your decision, and I'm proud of you, Miss Nellie O'Malley-All-Mended!"

❧

Nellie had made another decision, too, one that she had not told Miss Brennan about. That night, after everyone had gone to bed, Nellie slipped out from under the covers. She tiptoed to the bathroom, shut the door, and lit a candle. She took a sheet of paper, pen and ink, and an envelope from where she had hidden them in the linen closet.

Nellie addressed the envelope first. She wrote:

Clark School
Beacon Street
Boston, Massachusetts

Then she smoothed the sheet of paper flat. She began to write:

Dear Sirs,
I would like information about enrolling in your school.

On a lovely spring night about a week later, Uncle Gard, Aunt Cornelia, and Nellie were in the parlor reading. Bridget and Jenny had gone upstairs a while ago, lured to bed by the promise of a story from Samantha.

Aunt Cornelia looked at Uncle Gard. "Darling," she said in a worried voice. "You have such a long face. That letter you're reading is not from—" Aunt Cornelia stopped mid-sentence and glanced at Nellie.

"No, no," Uncle Gard said.

"Well, then," asked Aunt Cornelia, "is there bad news in the letter?"

Uncle Gard cleared his throat. "Well," he said. His voice sounded odd. "Well, this letter was addressed to the guardians of Miss Nellie O'Malley, so I opened it. It's from Clark School, in Boston. It says that Nellie is welcome to enroll there."

"What did you say?" asked Aunt Cornelia. "A school in Boston?"

Both Uncle Gard and Aunt Cornelia turned to Nellie. They looked hurt and confused. Nellie felt terrible. She had expected that the letter from Boston would be addressed to her, so she would see it first.

She had never meant to spring such a sad surprise on Uncle Gard and Aunt Cornelia.

Aunt Cornelia asked gently, "Is that . . . is that what you want, Nellie, to go away to school in Boston? Aren't you happy here with us?"

Nellie did not know how to explain that leaving seemed like the only way to save her friendship with Samantha and that, at the school in Boston, she could learn to be a teacher so that she could protect her sisters and keep her promise to Mam. She bent her head low. Just then, she heard a sound at the doorway. It was Samantha. Nellie looked at Samantha from under her bangs. From the look on Samantha's white and frozen face, Nellie knew that she had heard everything.

Nellie spoke quietly but firmly. She said, "I just think it would be best for everyone if I left."

TELLING
THE TRUTH

 Samantha turned sharply and ran back upstairs. "Nellie," Aunt Cornelia said in a soft, sad voice, "we'll talk all this over later. Right now, I think you had better go speak to Samantha."

Nellie rose slowly, and slowly she followed Samantha upstairs to their room. She dreaded the conversation that she knew she and Samantha must have.

Samantha was sitting on the window seat. The window was open, and a branch covered with pink blossoms looked bright in the darkness. It bobbed gracefully on the soft spring breeze.

Samantha faced Nellie. "So, you are going to

leave," she said flatly. Her voice sounded tired, as if all the life and hope had been drained out of it.

Nellie nodded.

"And will you take Bridget and Jenny with you?" Samantha asked.

"I'm responsible for them," Nellie said stiffly. "They are my sisters, even though they like you better than they like me."

"That's not true!" said Samantha.

"It's true that they're with you more than they're with me," said Nellie. "You tell them stories. You play with them. You put them to bed. They turn to *you* for comfort when they're sad or scared, not to *me*."

"I never meant to make you feel left out," said Samantha. "It's just that all my life I have wanted sisters. And I sort of thought that I was helping *you* by caring for Bridget and Jenny. You told me that it was hard for you to comfort them when they cried for your parents because you missed your parents so much yourself."

"Oh," said Nellie. Her jealousy began to melt away.

Samantha went on. "I know that I have been

spending a lot of time with Bridget and Jenny, especially since that day we went to the settlement house," she said. "When I saw the children there, I *hated* thinking of how you and Bridget and Jenny used to be poor and hungry like that . . ." Samantha's eyes filled with tears. "I just wanted to hug Bridget and Jenny and never let them go," she said. "I wanted to be with them every minute, to be sure that they were safe and happy."

"Samantha," Nellie began, "I—"

But Samantha interrupted. "I wished that I could help *all* the children at the settlement house and make their lives better, like Bridget's and Jenny's," she said, "and it made me sad and angry to know that I couldn't."

"Is that why you were crying in the cab when we came home from the settlement house?" asked Nellie.

Samantha nodded.

"I thought you hated the *settlement house*," said Nellie, "and that's why you never went back with Aunt Cornelia and me."

"Oh, no," said Samantha. "I wanted to go, but I thought it was a good thing to give you time

alone with Aunt Cornelia. I've tried to give you
time alone with Uncle Gard, too."

"You've been leaving me alone with them on
purpose?" asked Nellie.

"Yes," said Samantha. "I could tell that
something was bothering you. You weren't very
happy at school or here at home. You didn't seem
to want to talk to me about it. So I thought that
maybe if you were alone with Uncle Gard and
Aunt Cornelia, you'd tell *them* what was wrong."

"Oh, Samantha," said Nellie. "I don't know
whether to laugh or cry. I misunderstood you!
I was jealous of you and thought you were jealous
of me."

Samantha looked ashamed. In a low voice she
said, "I *was* jealous of you. I knew it was terrible of
me, but I couldn't help it. Everyone was always so
proud of you! And it . . . it sort of hurt my feelings
that you didn't seem to like our school anymore."

"I'm so sorry," said Nellie. "I could tell that I
was making you unhappy. I knew that I was
ruining our friendship so badly that the only thing
for me to do was to go away."

"Don't go, Nellie," Samantha begged.

"Please, *please*—don't go to Boston."

Nellie sighed. "I have to," she said. "I'll have to borrow money to buy a train ticket from Uncle Gard and Aunt Cornelia, but I'll pay them back every penny as soon as I can."

"But Uncle Gard and Aunt Cornelia love you," Samantha protested. "They want to adopt you and Bridget and Jenny and take care of you forever and ever. They told me so."

"Uncle Gard and Aunt Cornelia are good, kind people," said Nellie. "But I'm not sure that they'll be able to take care of us forever and ever."

"Why not?" asked Samantha.

"Because they're not our real parents," said Nellie.

"They're not *my* real parents, either!" exclaimed Samantha.

Nellie's heart twisted. Somehow, in the midst of all her troubles, she had forgotten that Samantha was an orphan, too.

Samantha spoke earnestly. "Don't you see, Nellie?" she asked. "We're trying to start a whole new family. It doesn't make any difference that

Aunt Cornelia and Uncle Gard are not your real aunt and uncle."

"Well, yes, I'm afraid it does," said Nellie. She decided that the time had come to tell Samantha the whole truth. "You were right when you thought that something was bothering me," she said. "I've had a terrible secret. You see, I saw my real uncle, Uncle Mike, on the street a few weeks ago. I ran away from him, but he said he would come find me. He said he would take Bridget and Jenny and me away with him. We'd have to work in the factory and give all our money to him."

Samantha gasped. "Why didn't you say something?" she asked.

"I didn't want everyone to worry," said Nellie. "And anyway, there didn't seem to be much point. I don't know how we can stop him from taking us if he wants to. He's our real uncle. He said we belong to him."

"So *that's* why you want to go to Boston," said Samantha. "To hide from your Uncle Mike so he can't find you."

"Yes," said Nellie. That *was* part of the reason. "But—"

"Nellie," Samantha interrupted, "you've been very brave. You're the bravest girl I know! But I think this problem with Uncle Mike is too big for you to handle by yourself. First thing tomorrow morning, let's tell Uncle Gard and Aunt Cornelia about Uncle Mike. I am sure that they can help."

"All right," said Nellie. She was not sure that *anyone* could help. She certainly did not see any way that Uncle Gard and Aunt Cornelia could stop Uncle Mike.

That night, for the first time in weeks, Nellie and Samantha talked late into the night. They knew Uncle Gard and Aunt Cornelia were talking to one another, too, because the grown-ups did not come up to tuck them in, at least not while Nellie and Samantha were still awake. The next morning when Nellie went down the stairs next to Samantha, she felt much happier than she had felt going up the night before. Samantha was her friend again, and that made everything better.

As Nellie and Samantha passed the door to the parlor, they heard voices. Nellie froze inside. She grabbed Samantha's hand.

"It's Uncle Mike!" Nellie whispered, horrified.

"He's found us. He's *here*. He . . . he's come to take us away!"

Samantha looked scared. She pulled Nellie away from the parlor. "What should we do?" she asked.

Nellie could feel that Samantha was trembling. She looked at Samantha's pale face and, suddenly, Nellie was furious. She could not bear to have Uncle Mike make Samantha scared. And she was tired of being afraid of him herself. Nellie squeezed Samantha's hand.

"I'm going in there to face him," she said. "I owe it to Bridget and Jenny, and to myself, too. I'll spend the rest of my life running away from him if I don't stand up to him right now."

Samantha bit her lip and nodded. "I'll come with you," she said.

Together, Samantha and Nellie went into the parlor.

Nellie took a deep breath. "Hello, Uncle Mike," she said.

Uncle Mike was slouched in a chair. He nodded to Nellie. "So, Nellie-girl," he said. "At last I've found you."

Uncle Gard spoke up. "That's not quite true," he said firmly to Uncle Mike. "*We* found *you*, Mr. O'Malley. You are here today because we asked you to come."

Uncle Mike growled, "Asked me to come, did you? More like you had that detective fellow chase me down and drag me here."

Nellie was astounded. She looked at Uncle Gard and Aunt Cornelia with a confused expression on her face. "But why?" she asked.

Aunt Cornelia came to Nellie and put her hands on Nellie's shoulders. "We have been looking for your uncle ever since you and your sisters came to live with us," she explained. "We've wanted to speak to him about adopting you and Bridget and Jenny."

Uncle Gard added, "Our detective finally found out where he was a few days ago. When you told us last night that you wanted to go to Boston, we thought we had better speak to him right away."

"So, Nellie-girl, you've been keeping secrets, have you?" said Uncle Mike. "You didn't tell these fine folks that you'd seen your dear old Uncle Mike weeks ago. You didn't tell them that I said that I'd find you and your sisters and take you back to live with me."

"No," said Nellie. "I didn't want to worry them."

Aunt Cornelia hugged Nellie. "Oh, you dear child!" she said. "No wonder you wanted to go to Boston! You wanted to hide from your uncle. Well, you need not worry any longer. We had the detective bring your uncle here today to settle everything. If you want to be adopted by us, we have papers for your uncle to sign to give up his rights to you and Bridget and Jenny."

"We will settle it so that you girls will live with us from now on," said Uncle Gard. "There are laws to protect children and to see to it that they're treated properly. Your Uncle Mike won't ever be able to take you away once he signs the legal agreement."

Uncle Mike crossed his arms over his chest. "I might sign the papers, or I might not," he said, full of bluster. "After all, the girls are the children of my dear late brother, and it would be a loss to me not to see them anymore. Of course, rich folks like you

"I wouldn't ask for money," Nellie said.
"I'd just sign the papers, if I were you."

could pay me to sign. How much money are Nellie-girl and her sisters worth to you?"

"How dare you, sir?" said Uncle Gard.

Nellie stepped forward so that she stood right in front of Uncle Mike. Uncle Gard had reminded her of what Miss Brennan had said about laws protecting children. "I wouldn't ask for money," Nellie said to Uncle Mike. "I'd just sign the papers, if I were you."

"Would you, now?" said Uncle Mike with a smirk.

"Yes," said Nellie coolly, "because if you don't sign, I promise you that I will tell everyone how you abandoned Bridget and Jenny and me and took all our money and left us to starve and freeze to death in January. I am sure it is against the law to treat children that way. I don't think any judge would let you have us back if he knew how mean you were to us. In fact, I bet you'd probably have to go to jail."

Uncle Mike's jaw hung open in shock. Then he snatched up the pen and scrawled his name on the papers. "It's good riddance to bad rubbish, is all I can say," he growled. He shoved his hat on his head and then shook his fist at them all as he left. "I hope I never see any of you ever again as long as I live!" he shouted.

For once, Nellie agreed with Uncle Mike wholeheartedly!

When the door slammed shut behind Uncle Mike, Aunt Cornelia and Uncle Gard collapsed into chairs. Samantha threw her arms around Nellie and hopped up and down, hugging her. "Oh, Nellie," she said. "You were wonderful! Oh, I'm so happy! Now you don't have to go to Boston."

But Nellie still looked solemn.

Uncle Gard pulled Nellie onto his lap, and Aunt Cornelia asked, "What's on your mind, Nellie?"

Nellie leaned back against Uncle Gard. It was harder to tell unhappy truths to kind people than to mean people like Uncle Mike, but she had to do it.

"Getting away from Uncle Mike wasn't the only reason I wanted to go to Boston," she said. "You see, I promised my mother that I would always take care of Bridget and Jenny. I thought that if I went to Clark School in Boston and learned to be a teacher, I could keep my promise to Mam.

Now I've realized that no matter what happens, I *still* want to be a teacher like Miss Brennan someday. I don't want to sound ungrateful. The school Samantha and I go to here in New York is very fine, but I don't think it is right for me. It's just not practical enough."

Aunt Cornelia smiled. "I understand," she said. "Let's ask Miss Brennan. I'm sure she'll know if there is a school like Clark School here in New York. If there is, we will enroll you there right away."

Samantha gave Nellie a playful poke. "You see?" she said with a grin. "You will be able to stay right here in New York and never do any more fluttery-arm dancing ever again!"

&

"Come on. Tell me!" said Nellie. "We promised each other that we wouldn't have any more secrets, remember?"

Samantha grinned. "I remember," she said.

It was a bright, sunshiny morning in May. Nellie and Samantha were on their way to school.

"At least give me a hint," coaxed Nellie.

"What's your secret wish about?"

"It's about my birthday," said Samantha, "which is only three weeks away!"

"That's pretty soon," said Nellie. "Oh, Samantha, please don't tell me that your secret birthday wish is for bloomers for me."

"No," said Samantha. "But my wish does have something to do with you."

Nellie looked so puzzled that Samantha laughed.

"All right," Samantha said. "I'll tell you. My secret wish is that your adoption will be final by my birthday. The present I'd like the most would be for Bridget and Jenny and you to be my sisters, really and truly."

"Really and truly and once and for all," said Nellie, smiling at her friend. "Yes, I'd like that, too."

The two girls stopped at the corner.

"Well, here's where we say good-bye," said Nellie. She and Samantha did not go to the same school anymore. Miss Brennan had known of the perfect school for Nellie, and Aunt Cornelia had enrolled Nellie in it immediately. Nellie loved her new school. It was very practical, and everything she learned there was useful.

"Good-bye, Nellie," said Samantha. "I'll see you later."

"Yes," said Nellie. "I'll see you at home." How she loved to say that!

Samantha skipped off toward her school. Nellie stood at the corner for a moment, watching her go. Samantha must have known that Nellie was watching her. Without turning around, Samantha waved good-bye. Nellie laughed out loud. Samantha was waving with a very fluttery arm.

LOOKING BACK

ADOPTION
IN
1906

Most young factory workers could only dream of life in a secure and comfortable home like Gard and Cornelia's.

Adjusting to a new and privileged life with Samantha after a life of hard work was more complicated than Nellie expected. And, as Nellie and Samantha discovered, the shift from being best friends to being sisters was not easy, either. It took tremendous love and determination to overcome the many obstacles that made it difficult for Nellie to be a part of Samantha's family.

Adoption between nonrelatives was rare in the early 1900s. Most families who were well-off enough to give poor children good homes would not have considered adopting a child "beneath their class." For the most part, families took care of their own, and social classes didn't mix. This system worked well for Samantha, who had

These three young orphans are standing in front of one of Chicago's largest orphanages.

loving and caring relatives. But it didn't work well for Nellie, whose uncle wanted her only because she could make money for him. There was no one to make sure that orphans like Nellie had decent homes and loving families. If a child was taken in by a blood relative, no questions were asked. Uncle Mike had abandoned Nellie and her sisters earlier, but he could reclaim them anytime he wanted. By law, the girls belonged to him forever. Although there was a growing movement of progressive people working to create laws to protect children like Nellie and her sisters, few such laws were in place in 1906.

Most children who ended up in orphanages were stuck there, forced into hard work to earn their keep until they became adults. "Orphan trains" offered one way out. These trains carried orphans out West to new homes and families. Some orphans were lucky

Each orphan was given one cardboard suitcase to hold his or her belongings on the trip west.

Notices like this were put up in advance in the towns along the orphan train route.

and were adopted by good families, but many orphans were separated from their brothers and sisters. And some adoptive families were really looking for farmhands, not sons and daughters.

Some children were sent West on the orphan trains by their own parents. Hoping for better lives for their children, parents unable to take care of them gave up all rights to their children by signing a legal contract called a "surrender form." By signing such a document, they made adoption by another family possible. A surrender form was the type of contract

At each station, the train stopped and the children filed out to be examined by local townspeople interested in adopting them.

that Gard and Cornelia would have asked Uncle Mike to sign. After Uncle Mike signed away his rights to the girls, Uncle Gard and Aunt Cornelia were free to start the process of legally adopting Nellie and her sisters.

The prospect of becoming sisters was complicated by the great divide in the social class system, and Nellie sometimes felt awkward in Samantha's world of wealth and privilege. Having been a servant in a wealthy household, Nellie knew only too well that many upper-class people believed it improper for the classes to mix. Some working-class people felt the same way, too. Nellie could tell that even Gertrude, Gard and Cornelia's maid, didn't like the idea of being a maid for girls who used to be servants themselves!

A girl like Nellie probably *would* have felt out of place in a fine private school like the one she attended with Samantha. Such schools prepared girls to become the wives of wealthy men rather than preparing them to work to support themselves. Nellie longed for a more

Nellie had more in common with other working-class girls like these than she did with the privileged girls at Samantha's school.

practical education so that she could get a good enough job to support herself and her sisters someday.

Miss Brennan had done exactly what Nellie hoped to be able to do—develop skills, make a new life, and help others. Special schools like Teachers College in New York City taught working-class women to become teachers. These schools offered important opportunities to move beyond the low-paying servant and factory jobs that kept immigrants and working-class people in poverty.

Many of those teachers went on to work in schools or in settlement houses, where they helped newly arrived immigrants adapt to life in America. In addition to lectures, art exhibits, and clubs, settlement houses offered classes for children and adults in American customs, English, cooking, math, and even dance. Settlement houses also had kindergartens and child-care

A settlement house cooking class

People of all ages enjoyed settlement house dance and music lessons. Teachers like Miss Brennan wanted people to have fun while they learned important skills.

facilities where mothers could leave their young children while they worked. Immigrants and neighborhood residents of all ages took advantage of settlement house services. There are still active settlement houses in some American cities today.

It was only after Nellie was certain Uncle Mike could no longer claim her and her sisters, and after she knew she would receive training to become a teacher, that she was able to turn to the important and joyful undertaking of fully becoming a sister to Samantha. Just as blended families today sometimes struggle to figure out how to become new families, Nellie and Samantha struggled. But they learned that by being honest, asking for help, and opening their hearts, they could find comfort, joy, and strength in their new family.

Learning to become sisters as well as friends brings extra joy in blended families today.

A SNEAK PEEK AT

MEET
Samantha

*Samantha Parkington can hardly wait to meet the
new girl who is moving in next door.*

amantha bounded into her backyard holding a gingerbread cookie. She took a deep breath of summer air and a couple of long leaps and stopped beside the tunnel.

The tunnel was a hole worn in the lilac hedge between her house and the Rylands', but Samantha had always called it "the tunnel." Through it now, she could see a girl. The girl was busy hanging laundry in the Rylands' yard. Could Eddie Ryland possibly have been telling the truth? Had this girl really come to live there? Samantha ducked through the tunnel and came closer.

"Are you Nellie?" she asked brightly.

The girl looked surprised and very timid. "Yes, miss," she answered without stopping her work. Eddie had said Nellie was nine, but this girl seemed smaller than Samantha.

"Are you visiting the Rylands?" asked Samantha.

This time Nellie looked amused. "Oh, no, miss. I'm working here," she said.

Samantha was surprised. Eddie hadn't said a girl was coming to *work*. But it didn't matter. Samantha thought it would be wonderful to have a friend right next door. She remembered the cookie in her hand. "Would you like some gingerbread?" she asked. "It's just baked."

Nellie looked at the Rylands' house. "Oh, no, miss. I can't."

"Won't they let you?" asked Samantha.

"No, I don't think so, miss. I've got my job to do," Nellie answered.

"My name's Samantha. You don't have to call me 'miss.'" Samantha put her cookie and napkin down on a stone and reached for a piece of wet laundry. "I'll help you, Nellie. Then we can play."

"Oh, no, you shouldn't," Nellie said. She was embarrassed, but there was nothing she could do to stop her new friend. So instead, she hurried to finish the job before anyone could see Samantha working.

When the last of the laundry was hung, Samantha grabbed Nellie's hand and pulled her toward the tunnel. "We can eat in here. Nobody will see us," Samantha said. The girls just fit into the hole in the hedge, and Nellie couldn't say no to the spicy smell of gingerbread.

"Why are you working here?" Samantha asked.

Nellie didn't look at Samantha when she answered. "My father works in a factory in the city, and my mother does washing. But there's three of us children, you see, and it's not enough." She added quietly, "There wasn't enough food. And there wasn't enough coal."

Samantha's eyes were wide with disbelief. She was good at imagining things, but she had never imagined hunger and cold. "You mean your parents sent you away? But that's awful!"

"Oh, no. It's better here. It really is," said Nellie. "The Rylands pay my family a dollar a week for the work I do. That's not as much as I earned in the factory, but in the factory I had to work every day but Sunday, until dark. And the air was so hot and dusty I started coughing a lot. That's why my parents let me come here. The air is good, and I don't have to work so long, and I get good food." With one finger, she collected the last of the cookie crumbs. "Only I don't get to see my family much."

Samantha was shocked into silence, but only for a moment. "When do you go to school?" she asked.

"I've never been to school," Nellie said quietly.

Was it possible? This girl had never gone to

school? Samantha's mind raced. "Nellie, I have an idea," she said. "We can meet here every day, and I'll teach you. The Rylands won't miss you for just a little while, and I'll teach you *everything.*"

Nellie's eyes glittered with excitement as the girls made plans. Then Samantha began talking about everyone she lived with and all the neighbors. By the time she told Nellie about Uncle Gard's motorcar, they were both giggling.

The girls were interrupted by a familiar voice. "I see you, Samantha! I see you, Nellie!"

"Eddie, get out of here," Samantha snapped.

"I'm telling!"

Nellie jumped up. "I'd better get back to work," she said.

Samantha followed her out of the tunnel. "All right. But tomorrow we'll make a telephone. Mrs. Hawkins will give us two tin cans, and I can get a string. We'll string it through the hedge, where Eddie won't see it. Then we can talk whenever we want to. Oh, Nellie, we'll have the most wonderful time!"

READ ALL OF SAMANTHA'S STORIES,
available at bookstores and *americangirl.com*.

MEET SAMANTHA • An American Girl
Samantha becomes good friends with Nellie, a servant girl,
and together they plan a secret midnight adventure.

SAMANTHA LEARNS A LESSON • A School Story
Samantha becomes Nellie's teacher, but Nellie has some
very important lessons to teach Samantha, too.

SAMANTHA'S SURPRISE • A Christmas Story
Uncle Gard's friend Cornelia is ruining Samantha's
Christmas. But Christmas morning brings surprises!

HAPPY BIRTHDAY, SAMANTHA! • A Springtime Story
When Eddie Ryland spoils Samantha's birthday party,
Cornelia's twin sisters know just what to do.

SAMANTHA SAVES THE DAY • A Summer Story
Samantha enjoys a peaceful summer at Piney Point,
until a terrible storm strands her on Teardrop Island!

CHANGES FOR SAMANTHA • A Winter Story
When Samantha finds out that her friend Nellie is living in an
orphanage, she must think of a way to help her escape.

◆

WELCOME TO SAMANTHA'S WORLD • 1904
American history is lavishly illustrated
with photographs, illustrations, and
excerpts from real girls' letters and diaries.